I WONDER

I WONDER

Celebrating Daddies Doin' Work

Doyin Richards

Feiwel and Friends
NEW YORK

A Feiwel and Friends Book

An Imprint of Macmillan

Printed in China by Toppan Leefung Printing Ltd., Dongguan City, Guangdong Province.
For information, address Feiwel and Friends, 175 Fifth Avenue, New York, N.Y. 10010.

Our books may be purchased in bulk for promotional, educational, or business use.
Please contact your local bookseller or the Macmillan Corporate and Premium Sales Department
at (800) 221-7945 ext. 5442 or by e-mail at MacmillanSpecialMarkets@macmillan.com.

Library of Congress Cataloging-in-Publication Data is available.

ISBN 978-1-250-07895-7 (hardcover)

Book design by Anna Booth

Feiwel and Friends logo designed by Filomena Tuosto

First Edition—2016

The photos in this book were gathered by the author from his followers on Instagram and are used with permission.

10 9 8 7 6 5 4 3 2 1

mackids.com

Doyin (center) with his brothers, Femi and Shola.

My dad, Femi Richards, is the greatest man I know, and I easily could have dedicated this book to him, but I decided to take a different approach. *I Wonder* provides a glimpse into the world of modern fatherhood, and my two brothers understand the rewards and challenges that dads face today better than anyone.

As the baby of the family by a mere sixty-two seconds, I always admired my older brother Femi Richards Jr. and my identical twin, Shola Richards—but my admiration was taken to another level when they became fathers. Both are successful corporate executives, but they believe without a shadow of a doubt that the most important job title they will ever have is Dad. They are nurturing, loving, present, supportive, patient, and everything I aspire to be as I navigate through fatherhood.

Fellas, I don't tell you this enough, but there's no chance I would be the dad I am today without you showing me the ropes. Your kids are incredibly lucky to be raised by you, and I'm incredibly lucky to have the best brothers imaginable to learn from.

I love you both very much. Keep Doin' Work.

HELLO, LITTLE ONE.

I am so happy you are here with me.

Every moment we spend together is an adventure. We laugh. We eat. We play games.

And sometimes we just do nothing at all.

But there are times when I start to wonder.

I WONDER

if you think I push you too high on the swing set. I do it because you're a star and I want you to see the sky up close.

I WONDER if you like the ponytail I created for you. I know it's a little bumpy, but I'm trying. With a little practice, I'll be the best stylist this neighborhood has ever seen.

I WONDER

if you like my silly voices when I read to you. I do it because I want you to use your imagination to know that anything can come to life as long as you want it to.

I WONDER

if you think I'm being too hard on you when I tell you to never give up. I do it because I know you have the toughness within you to do anything.

I WONDER if you understand why I want you to focus more on inner beauty. I do it because I know being good-looking doesn't mean much unless you are kind and smart.

I WONDER if you're scared when I ask you to try new things. I do it because I want you to experience the great, big world around you.

I WONDER if you understand why I don't spend big money on material items...you know... "stuff." I do it because I spend it on experiences that will create lifelong memories.

I WONDER if you're tired of the countless photos I take with you. I have them because each picture serves as a priceless treasure capturing a moment in time. A moment that I can hold in my hands and cherish forever.

I WONDER if you enjoy seeing me work my magic in the kitchen. I do it because I want you to know that it's normal and expected for a dad to prepare meals for his kids.

I WONDER if you think about me as much as I think about you when we're not together. If I could create a machine to teleport to you, I would in an instant just to hold your hand.

I WONDER if you notice how often I watch you sleep. I do it because you're growing so fast and I want to keep you young forever.

But one thing
I never wonder
about is
how much
I **LOVE YOU**.

If you need a
cheerleader in
the front row...

a shoulder to cry on
when you're feeling low . . .

an audience when you need to "go"...

a partner
to roll
around in
the grass
or snow . . .

a companion
to watch the
bubbles blow...

a dancer for your music show...

or a motivator when you
feel the doubts grow...

I will **always** be there for you.
In **all ways. Expect** that.

Every day I thank my lucky stars for being chosen to be a part of your life.

So I **WONDER**, little one.
Do you feel the same way
about me?

And then, with a flash of your smile and the grip of your hug, I know that you do.